How Many Ways Can You Cook an Egg?

For Ezra; my recipe stress-tester, and my littlest, most vocal critic. I hope the dinner dances never end – L.M.

To my father, for his unconditional love and support, and teaching me how to flip pancakes, to my sister, for guiding the way to crazy adventures and heaps of dumplings, and to Frederik, thanks for always rooting for me. I love you and your quesadillas – C.D.

BIG PICTURE PRESS

First published in the UK in 2022 by Big Picture Press,
an imprint of Bonnier Books UK
4th Floor, Victoria House
Bloomsbury Square, London WC1B 4DA
Owned by Bonnier Books
Sveavägen 56, Stockholm, Sweden
www.bonnierbooks.co.uk

Consulted by Sophie Lennon at FeedEatGrow

1 3 5 7 9 10 8 6 4 2

MIX
Paper from
responsible sources
FSC® C104723

ISBN 978 1 80078 116 0

This book was typeset in Obnoxious Tie, Archer and Oranges and Lemons.
The illustrations were created with pencil and coloured digitally.

Designed by Olivia Cook
Edited by Joanna McInerney
Production by Nick Read

Printed in China

How Many Ways Can You Cook an Egg?

Fun-filled **RECIPES** for all the family

LIZZIE MABBOTT

Illustrated by
CHARLOTTE DUMORTIER

BPP

CONTENTS

A Letter for Big People   6
Health and Safety   7
Tips and Techniques   8
Perfecting your Slicing   9

FRUIT

The World of Fruit   12
All About Apples   14
Apple and Sultana Pancakes with Cinnamon Butter   16
Apple, Onion and Sage Relish   18
Apple, Blackberry and Hazelnut Turnovers   20

FROM THE GARDEN

Roots, Nightshades, Leafy Greens and Stems   24
Green Sauces of the World   26
Pesto   27
All About Fungi   28
All About Pulses and Corn   30
Sweetcorn Fritters   32
Mexican Street Corn   33
Cheesy Polenta and Fries   34
Cornbread   35
Challenge! Fermenting Vegetables   36

FROM THE OCEAN

All About Fish   40
How Many Ways Can You Cook a Fish?   42
Chinese Steamed Fish Pouches   44
Spiced Fish Fingers   46
Challenge! The Cornershop   48

FROM THE LAND

The World of Meat   52

How Many Ways Can You Cook a Chicken?   54

Brick Chicken   56

Phở Gà   57

Chicken Curry   58

Challenge! Meat on Sticks   60

DAIRY AND EGGS

All About Dairy and Eggs   64

How Many Ways Can You Cook an Egg?   66

Menemen   68

Custard   69

Quiche   70

Challenge! Ultimate Cheesy Toastie   72

PASTA, NOODLES AND DUMPLINGS

The World of Pasta and Noodles   76

All About Dumplings   78

One-Pot Pasta   80

Sesame Peanut Noodles   81

Beijing-Style Dumplings with Dipping Sauce   82

Challenge! Making Noodles   84

GRAINS AND BREADS

The World of Grains   88

All About Rice   90

Egg-Fried Rice   92

Tahdig   93

Baked Rice Pudding   94

About the Author and Illustrator   96

A Letter for Big People

Food is such an integral part of our lives – one might argue the *most* integral – and this book was written with the intention of turning what seem like daily chores such as shopping and cooking, into fun and inclusive activities for all the family. Fast food, quick and easy midweek meals and convenience foods are incredibly popular for our busy lifestyles, but what if the experience wasn't just in the eating of food? What if we extended that enjoyment to the sourcing of ingredients, researching of recipes and experimenting with flavours? That's what this book is all about.

Food hits all the senses: sight, smell, taste, feel, and the sounds of crispy, crunchy, soft and squishy... And finally, the satisfied "mmmmmmh!" that will erupt from your little people's mouths on first taste, is what makes cooking so enjoyable.

Mistakes and mishaps are often made while cooking, no matter how experienced you are – pastry rips, custard curdles, pasta boils over. Celebrate mistakes with your little one, patch them up as best you can, and don't dwell on them – there is a certain degree of resilience one acquires when things go wrong. It's all part of the learning process! But most of all, have fun!

Lizzie Mabbott

Health and Safety

Safety guidelines are included with most recipes, but it's advisable to talk to your little ones about basic health and safety before you get started. Please be on hand to help them with anything they're nervous of, and if you don't feel comfortable with them handling a certain utensil or something hot, always err on the side of caution. The main things to consider are:

Hygiene Make sure hands are thoroughly washed before cooking and tie back long hair.

Allergies If you have allergies or you are cooking for someone who does, always use ingredients that are safe.

Raw food Wash hands and surfaces with warm, soapy water after handling raw meat, seafood and eggs. Fruit and vegetables should also be washed.

Fridge storage It is advisable to arrange your fridge with raw meat and seafood on the bottom shelf, vegetables and fruit in drawers and cooked food or ingredients that don't need cooking above.

Freshness Both raw and cooked food should be adequately wrapped.

Sharp objects All cutting, slicing and chopping should be done under adult supervision. Only you will know how proficient your little one is with handling sharp objects like knives, peelers and cheese graters.

Heat When dealing with hot pans and oil, it's advised that children wear long sleeves and closed-toe shoes and are supervised at all times. Additionally, please help your little ones with handling anything from the oven that is hot – particular care should be taken that oven gloves aren't wet or damp when they're being used, as this can cause steam burns.

1

Tips and Techniques

This book is all about getting involved in the kitchen! Don't be afraid to get stuck in. Below are some of the techniques you will need to know.

Beat

Mix

Grate

Simmer

Sift

Whisk

How to knead

To knead dough, first make a ball and then gently push your palm into it, stretching the dough apart a little. Then, turn and do it again. Keep turning, rotating and pushing.

Perfecting Your Slicing

A gentle introduction to cutting and slicing is encouraged, and there are many brands of knife suitable for children from 18 months to get them started safely.

Julienne

This is also known as the matchstick cut, as the slices should be thin. You will need a sharp knife for this technique, or you can use a julienne peeler. Take your time and aim for even pieces.

Diced

Dicing means to chop into even bite-size cubes. Big People, don't hesitate to give uneven vegetables a quick once-over with a sharper knife once your little person has moved on to the next task – it will make for an easier cooking experience.

Sliced

A sharp knife will help to achieve a nice thin, even slice, but none of the recipes will taste horrible if this isn't achieved.

THE WORLD OF FRUIT

Fruit is nature's sugar, providing us with little bursts of energy and sweetness. The most exciting thing about fruit is the sheer variety of flavours, textures and ways they can be enjoyed. So many make a wonderful snack on the go, but some definitely need cooking before they become palatable – I'm looking at you, quince!

Soft Fruit

These fruits are normally small, squishy and stoneless.

Strawberry

Blueberry

Gooseberry

Raspberry

Blackberry

Grapes

Pomegranate

Kiwi

Persimmon

Pome Fruit

Pome fruits are produced by flowering trees.

Apple

Pear

Quince

Melons

Melons are round, sweet fruits with tough skins. Always tap your melons! If they sound hollow, they're perfectly ripe.

Charentais

Galia Melon

Cantaloupe

Watermelon

Honeydew Melon

Winter Melon

Bitter Melon

Stone Fruit

With a few exceptions such as mangoes, stone fruits rarely ripen once picked, which makes it doubly important to eat them at the height of their season.

Mango

Cherries

Plum

Nectarine

Lemon

Orange

Lime

Citrus Fruit

Citrus fruits are juicy, sharp, fragrant, sweet and honeyed.

Bergamot

Grapefruit

Tangerine

Kumquat

Guava

Banana

Dragon fruit

Tomato

Lychee

Rambutan

Tropical Fruit

These delicious fruits grow on trees found in the tropics.

Pineapple

Jackfruit

Star fruit

Fruit you might think are vegetables but are actually BERRIES!

Avocado

Aubergine

Juicy, squidgy, crisp, crunchy, gooey, slimy, tart, bitter, sweet, floral – everything is covered in the world of fruit. No two experiences will taste the same, either: a peach, bitten into on a sun-soaked day with juice running down your arm won't compare to a peach cobbler, baked until bubbling and drenched with custard. Therein lies the beauty – eat with the seasons and you will never be bored.

ALL ABOUT APPLES

Although some apples are in season all year round, many of them are at their best when the leaves on the trees start to turn brown and the temperature cools. Crunchy, shiny, crisp, juicy apples make a welcome change to the often heavy, warming food of the colder months. But apples baked into pies and puddings are soft and comforting and are a delicious way to greet the autumn season.

Granny Smith

MOST TART

Pink Lady

Red Prince

Bramley

Braeburn

To get the best from your apples when cooking, you need to get to grips with their individual flavours and textures. Hard, dense Bramley or Braeburn apples hold on to their juices well, so they are best-suited to chopping and cooking until soft. Perky Cox or Gala apples are sweet and fragrant, so they are great for snacking on, or adding raw to salads or bircher muesli.

Experiment with combining a couple of different apples when cooking for more interesting flavours. If you're able, shopping at loose-pick greengrocers means you can buy a wider variety.

MOST SWEET

Royal Gala

Opal

Red Delicious

Jazz

Egremont Russet

Golden Delicious

Cox

DID YOU KNOW?
The world's heaviest apple was recorded in 2005 in Japan, weighing an enormous 1.849kg (4lb 1oz). That's three times heavier than a basketball!

Apple and Sultana Pancakes with Cinnamon Butter

MAKES 8 PANCAKES

50g (¼ cup) sultanas, soaked in 50ml (1 ½ fl. oz.) boiling water for 15 mins

2 apples of your choosing; Pink Lady and Egremont Russet work well here

80g (¾ cup) plain flour

40g (⅓ cup) wholemeal flour

1 ½ tsp baking powder

1 medium egg

80ml (2 ⅔ fl. oz.) whole milk

2 tsp cinnamon

1 tbsp caster sugar (optional)

100g (~½ cup) unsalted butter (at room temperature)

These warm, fluffy pillow-y pancakes are not only great with apples, but you can also mix them with other fruit to match the seasons. Poached pears, blood oranges with honey, roasted plums with almonds – once you know the basics of how to make a pancake, you can really branch out. Experiment with different spices in the butter too, like nutmeg or ground ginger.

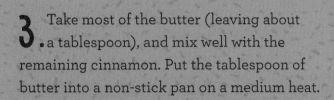

1. Peel and core the apples, then grate one on the largest side of the box grater, and cube the other into small dice. Toss the cubes with half the cinnamon and set to one side. Add the grated apple to a large mixing bowl with the drained sultanas.

2. To make the batter, add the egg and milk to the mixing bowl, then give it a good stir. Sift in the baking powder, sugar (if using), plain and wholemeal flours, and mix together.

3. Take most of the butter (leaving about a tablespoon), and mix well with the remaining cinnamon. Put the tablespoon of butter into a non-stick pan on a medium heat.

4. Using a ladle, add the batter to the pan. The portion should be about the size of a Big Person's fist. Turn the heat down to medium-low, and watch the bubbles break the surface of the pancake. When the top is looking nice and bubbled (after around 2 minutes), gently flip the pancake using a spatula, or if you're

BIG PERSON TIP
*These are great for children who are
learning to grip and feed themselves,
but can also be enjoyed by the whole
family on a lazy Sunday morning.*

feeling brave, by tossing the pancake up in
the air and catching it in the pan. To do this,
loosen the pancake around the edges with your
spatula, give it a shuffle by moving the pan back
and forth, and in one smooth and confident
movement, lift the pan, tilt it slightly towards
you and flick your wrist. Then hope for the best!

5. If you have a large pan you can make 2 or 3
pancakes at a time. Move to a plate and
leave in a warm oven while you make the rest.

6. To serve, add a smudge of cinnamon
butter over the pancake and top with
the cubed apple. Serve with syrup if you've
got an energetic day ahead of you!

Apple, Onion and Sage Relish

2 BIG PEOPLE & 2 LITTLE PEOPLE (AS A SIDE DISH)

2 Granny Smith apples, cored and cut into small cubes

2 bowls of ice-cold water, one with a **little lemon juice** squeezed into it

1 white onion, peeled and diced finely

A pinch of salt

6 sage leaves

1 tbsp butter

The sharpness of the Granny Smith apple is perfect for accompanying rich flavours, such as cheese, nuts, sausages and roast pork. This tangy relish also works wonderfully with black pudding and *morcilla*, which are mildly flavoured and warm with spices. This relish can also be cooked – just swap the Granny Smith with a more appropriate Bramley or Braeburn, and stew on a low heat with a drop of water for a softer, jammier sauce. It's the perfect accompaniment to a lovely Sunday roast with all the family!

1. Add the diced onion to a bowl of ice-cold water for at least 15 mins. This technique takes some of the raw harshness away.

2. Add the cubed apple to the bowl of ice water with lemon – this prevents the apple turning brown.

4. Drain the diced onion and pat dry, then add to the buttery pan. Give the onion a good swivel around before adding to a clean bowl.

3. In a small frying pan, add the butter and when foaming, add the sage leaves. Turn the leaves occasionally, frying until crisp but not blackened. Remove and drain on a piece of kitchen paper.

5. Drain the apple, pat dry and then add to the onion. Crumble the sage leaves into the bowl as well. Add the salt and toss gently with your hands.

Apple, Blackberry and Hazelnut Turnovers

MAKES 4 TURNOVERS

1 puff pastry sheet

1 large Bramley or Braeburn apple, peeled, cored and cubed

120g (½ cup) fresh blackberries

1 tsp caster sugar

3 tsp cornflour

3 tbsp finely chopped hazelnuts or almonds

Flaked almonds (optional)

1 large egg separated into yolk and white

1 tbsp milk

You can use shop-bought pastry to make these turnovers, but if you've got some time on your hands, making your own flaky rough-puff will be even better. The smell of pastry crisping and apple stewing will fill your home like a big hug. These delicious turnovers are happily eaten on their own, but they also make a great dessert, especially when served with ice cream or warm custard.

1. Preheat the oven to 200°C (400°F).

2. Lay the puff pastry sheet onto a baking tray lined with greaseproof paper. Whip the egg white with a fork until bubbles appear. Using a pastry brush, sweep the egg white over the pastry and place in the fridge for 15 minutes. This provides a barrier between the pastry and the fruit, minimising the risk of soggy bottoms.

3. To make the filling, toss the apple with the caster sugar and cornflour in a bowl, and then add the blackberries. Stir in the hazelnuts gently.

4. Cut the pastry sheet into four large squares, and draw a line diagonally across each lightly with a butter knife – you don't want to cut it, but it's helpful to mark where the filling should go.

5. Add 2 tbsp of filling to one side of the square, and then fold the turnover at the half fold. Then, seal that pastry well! Either crimp the edges with a fork, or you can get fancy and pinch seal – press your forefinger into the pastry, then use your forefinger and thumb on the opposite hand to squeeze the pastry on either side. Repeat all along the edge. Do the same thing for each turnover.

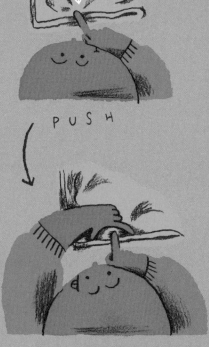

PUSH

PUT INDEX & THUMB OVER FINGER

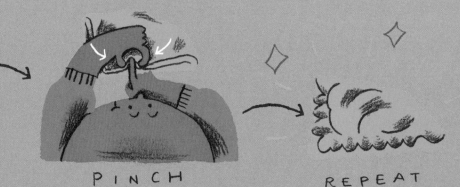

PINCH

REPEAT

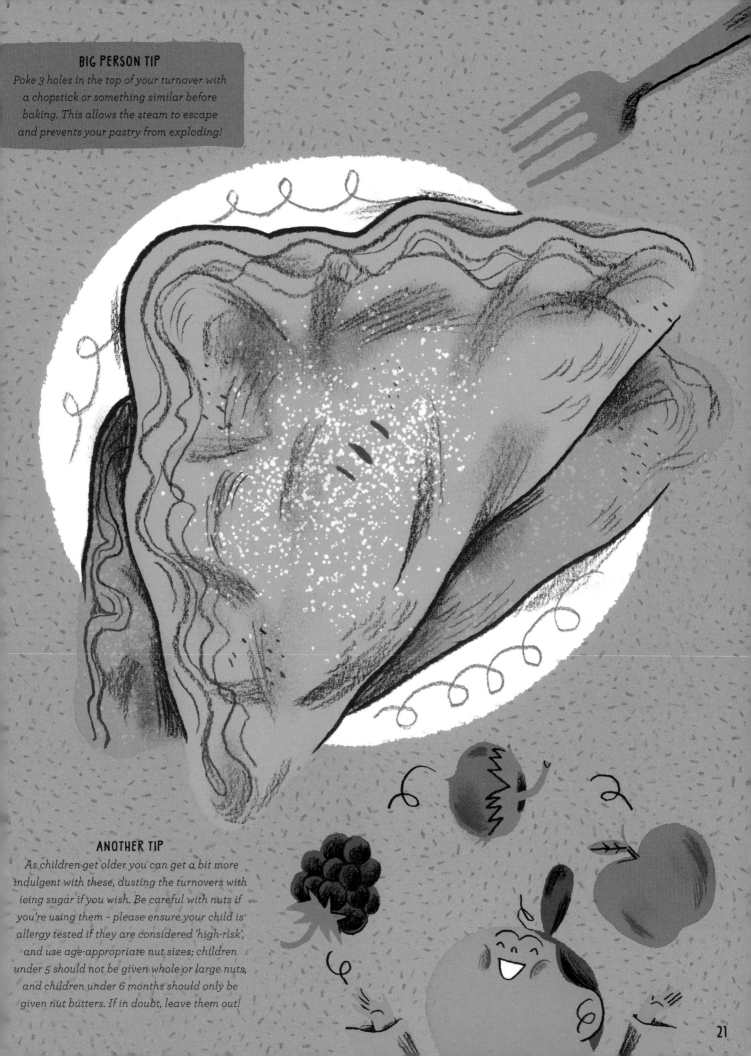

Poke 3 holes in the top of your turnover with a chopstick or something similar before baking. This allows the steam to escape and prevents your pastry from exploding!

ANOTHER TIP
As children get older you can get a bit more indulgent with these, dusting the turnovers with icing sugar if you wish. Be careful with nuts if you're using them – please ensure your child is allergy tested if they are considered 'high-risk', and use age-appropriate nut sizes; children under 5 should not be given whole or large nuts, and children under 6 months should only be given nut butters. If in doubt, leave them out!

21

FROM
THE
GARDEN

Roots, Nightshades, Leafy Greens and Stems

The world of vegetables is vast and inspiring, and every season new delights arrive. Over the course of a growing year it's possible to eat the entire rainbow — it's sometimes hard to believe that all of these colourful beauties grow in soil.

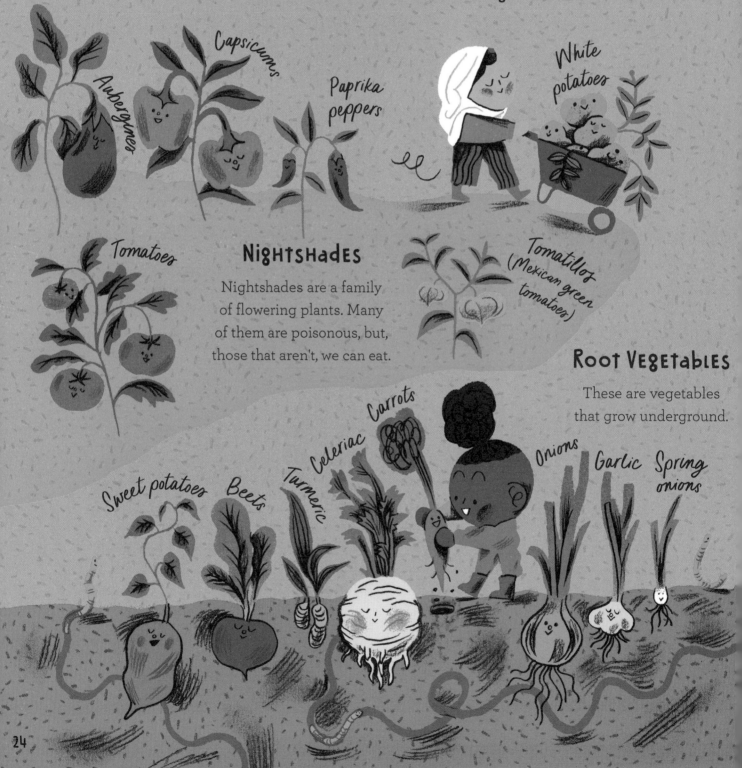

Aubergines

Capsicums

Paprika peppers

White potatoes

Tomatoes

Nightshades

Nightshades are a family of flowering plants. Many of them are poisonous, but, those that aren't, we can eat.

Tomatillos (Mexican green tomatoes)

Root Vegetables

These are vegetables that grow underground.

Carrots

Celeriac

Turmeric

Beets

Sweet potatoes

Onions

Garlic

Spring onions

Carrot

Broccoli

Cauliflower

Bok choy

Leek

Fennel

Celery

Kohlrabi

Swiss chard

CRUCIFEROUS

Be warned: these vegetables contain sugars that can make you gassy. Parp!

Brussels sprouts

Radishes

Kale

Asparagus

STEMS

In this group, the plant stalks are the edible bits.

Rhubarb

BEANS

We eat many types of cooked dried beans (see page 30), but these ones are best eaten fresh.

Runner beans

Broad beans

French beans

Peas

Edamame

Mangetout

25

Green Sauces of the World

These green sauces are marvellously easy to make. Simply whizz in a blender, or put everything into a bowl and stir in your wet ingredients, like oil and vinegar. Below is a selection from around the world. How many can you make?

Zhoug
This Middle-Eastern sauce is made from coriander, cardamom, garlic, cumin and jalapeños.

Mint Sauce
English mint sauce is made from mint, white wine vinegar and caster sugar.

Salsa Verde
This zingy sauce from Mexico uses coriander, tomatillos, garlic and lime.

Green Chutney
This warming chutney is from India. It uses mint, coriander, green chilli, cumin, roasted nuts and gram flour.

Green Goddess
This is an American sauce. It's made from parsley, tarragon, chives, Greek yoghurt, garlic, lemon, anchovies and capers.

Grüne Sosse
This is German, and means 'green sauce'. It's made from parsley, cress, salad burnet, borage, sorrel, chives, chervil, cooked egg yolks and sour cream.

Coriander

Mint

Chives

Tarragon

Parsley

Sorrel

Chervil

Pesto

A Big Person's handful of basil leaves

Parmesan cheese

A dash of pine nuts

A splash of extra virgin olive oil

1 garlic clove, crushed

A pinch of salt and pepper (optional)

Pesto is easy to make – all you have to do is throw the ingredients in a blender! However, there are some people who believe that pesto must be bashed in a pestle and mortar for the best flavour, and others might be upset that their sauce hasn't been chopped by hand. If you want to practise your chopping action, start with the hardest items first – for example garlic and nuts – and then work your way up to the softest, like basil leaves. Just keep chop, chop, chopping away.

1. Place the basil leaves and pine nuts into a blender or food processor, and pulse until you create a thick paste.

2. Add the crushed garlic clove and parmesan cheese, then blend again.

3. As you blend, slowly add the extra virgin olive oil.

4. Add salt and pepper to taste.

BIG PERSON TIP
Many adults and children have too much salt in their diet. Keeping added salt to a minimum is advised.

ALL ABOUT FUNGI

There are millions of different types of mushrooms. There are cute ones, like 'hairy parachute' and 'lemon disco' and there are some downright scary ones, like 'death cap'. Mushroom foraging is a popular activity, but you absolutely must not pick or eat any mushrooms you've found growing in the wild. They can range from perfectly edible to deadly poisonous, and it's incredibly hard to tell them apart, so only experts should pick them.

Here are some delicious edible mushrooms. Many are seasonal, so you may not be able to find them all year round. Autumn is a particularly great time of year for many mushrooms:

Oyster

Chanterelle

Snow fungus

Beech

White shimeji

White

Chicken of the woods

Enoki

Shiitake

Morel

Mushrooms contain glutamate, which gives an 'umami' taste (and is super fun to say – oooh-mah-me). This is a deeply savoury flavour that occurs naturally in tomatoes, anchovies and cheese.

Penny bun

Portobello

ALL ABOUT PULSES...

Loosely speaking, anything you find in the dried bean and lentil section of the supermarket is likely to be called a pulse. Pulses are grown and eaten all over the world, and are nutritious both for soil health and our own.

Adzuki beans are often cooked into a puree and sweetened for desserts in both Japan and China.

Adzuki bean

Red lentil

Mung bean

In Hong Kong, green bean (**mung bean**) and red bean ice lollies are a common sight.

Marrowfat peas are cooked down into 'mushy peas' and often served with fish and chips.

Marrowfat pea

Split lentils are used a lot in South Asian cooking. They are called 'dal' – which is also the name of the dish they're made into.

Green Lentil (Puy)

Kidney bean

Black-eyed pea

White bean (including baked beans!)

Chickpea

Chickpeas are an important ingredient in the Middle East – hummus is made with just the addition of garlic, salt, tahini, lemon juice and olive oil.

QUICK COOK IDEA

For quick and easy ice lollies, blend together 1 drained tin of cooked adzuki beans (reserving 2 tbsp of whole beans) with ½ tin of coconut milk and 3 prunes. Stir in the beans, then place in ice lolly moulds and freeze overnight.

...and Corn

Corn is an ancient grain (read more about grains on pages 88–89), first used over 10,000 years ago in Mexico. It is grown all over the world and its uses from fresh to dried are extremely wide-ranging. Corn feeds a huge number of the world's population across the Americas and Africa. There are three main types:

Sweetcorn

Sweetcorn can be eaten fresh as corn on the cob, but also comes frozen and in tins.

Popcorn

Not all dried corn kernels can make popcorn, in fact only one variety will pop!

Ground Corn

Corn can be ground down to various textures, and is often eaten as porridge – known as grits in North America – or as polenta (see page 34). It is also used to make flour; *Masa harina* is a Mexican flour with a distinctive corn flavour. It's used to make tacos and tortilla chips.

DID YOU KNOW?

Quetzalcóatl was one of the most important ancient deities of Mesoamerica (the historic name for Central America); he was the God of Creation, and legend has it that he, disguised as an ant, discovered corn with which to feed people!

SWEETCORN FRITTERS

MAKES 9–12 FRITTERS

1 corn on the cob, husked and kernels shaved off *or*
1 can of tinned sweetcorn, 160g (1 cup) when drained (you can also use frozen sweetcorn, covered with boiling water for 2 mins, then drained well)

2 spring onions, finely sliced

1 small handful of coriander leaves and stalks, finely chopped

A pinch of salt (optional)

20ml (~1fl. oz.) milk

1 medium egg

2 tbsp self-raising flour

1 tbsp cooking oil

Get ready for a riot of flavour in these fritters! They are super adaptable and you can try many tasty experiments to get the combination you like. For example, swap parsley for coriander if you're not keen, or add a sliced chilli if you feel like you need some heat dancing on your tongue. Even the sweetcorn can be replaced. Grated courgette, sweet potato or beetroot work really well here too (though the latter might stain your hands – and everything else – purple for a while!).

TOP TIP

Serve these with one or a few of the following: guacamole, roasted cherry tomatoes on the vine, fried/poached eggs, crisp streaky bacon, sweet chilli jam

1. In a large mixing bowl, add the corn, spring onions, coriander, salt, milk and egg. Mix well so that the egg is nicely beaten, then add 1 tbsp of self-raising flour and mix again. Gradually add more of the flour and continue to mix until you have a batter that is thick with corn, droppable consistency and not too gluey. Your spoon should be able to move through the mixture with ease.

2. Put a non-stick pan on a medium heat, and warm the oil until it's hot and shimmering. Drop the corn batter in carefully, (a couple of tablespoons), and watch closely. After around 2 or 3 minutes, the edges will start to firm up and bubbles will form on top. At that point, use a spatula to gently lift and turn the fritter, and cook for another 3 to 4 minutes.

Mexican Street Corn

SERVES 2 LITTLE PEOPLE

1 corn on the cob, husked, and snapped in half

2 tbsp mayonnaise

60g (~½ cup) grated *cotija* (or a hard salty cheese like feta works well)

1 lime

½ tsp chilli powder (optional)

Coriander to serve

This is a wonderful way to eat corn – salty, sour and sweet flavours all combined – and best eaten on a hot summer's day, maybe around a barbecue, with plenty of napkins to hand. If you don't cover your nose in cheese and mayonnaise, you're not eating it right!

1. With a Big Person's help, grill or barbecue your corn cobs, turning so that it browns and chars evenly.

2. Leave to cool slightly. Then, using a pastry brush, liberally brush the mayonnaise on top, sprinkle with cheese and dust with chilli powder (if using).

3. Cut open the lime, and squeeze the juice over with a flourish. Scatter the coriander on top just before eating.

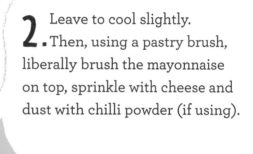

CHeesy PoLeNta and FRies

SERVES 2 BIG PEOPLE
& 2 LITTLE PEOPLE,
PLUS LEFTOVERS

250g (1 ½ cups) of
instant polenta

1l (~35fl. oz.) water with
vegetable or chicken stock

15g (1 tbsp) unsalted butter

**A handful of your favourite
cheese** – Parmesan, Grana
Padano, Cheddar, Comté
or Gruyère work well.
Or Gorgonzola if you're
feeling like a rich meal.

Polenta is made from dried corn that has been ground to a fine powder. From Northern Italy, it is a moisture sucker, so it has to be cooked long and slow and stirred frequently, unless you're using instant. It can be served as a texture similar to softly scrambled eggs alongside sausages and onion gravy, hearty stews or ragouts. As soon as polenta cools, it forms a cake and that's when it can be made into delicious cheesy fries – more on them below!

1. Add the liquid to a large saucepan and bring it to a high heat. When bubbling turn it down low, and using a whisk, start whisking the water. Please wear oven gloves for extra safety to prevent any splashes! Ask your Big Person to pour the polenta into the saucepan in a slow, steady stream, while you whisk.

2. Still whisking, bring this mixture to the boil until the polenta becomes thick and starts to spit. Lower the heat immediately, and this is where the workout begins!

3. Whisk for 5 full minutes – it might be a good idea to swap with your kitchen helper every minute or so, as your arms will get tired!

4. Stir in the butter and cheese and serve immediately. Once you have portioned all you need, pour any leftovers into a large container – as soon as polenta cools, it sets into a cake so it's much easier to manage when it's still warm.

FoR poLeNta FRies:

1. Turn your leftover polenta out onto a chopping board.

2. Slice into triangles, wedges or rectangles and dab dry with kitchen towel.

3. In a non-stick pan, add a drizzle of cooking oil on a medium heat, and when shimmering, carefully add the polenta pieces and fry on each side until they are golden and crisp. This takes around 10 minutes per side.

Cornbread

SERVES 2 BIG PEOPLE & 2 LITTLE PEOPLE

240g (1 ½ cups) coarse cornmeal or polenta

50g (½ cup) strong bread flour

1 tsp table salt

2 tsp caster sugar

2 medium eggs

480g (~2 cups) natural yoghurt

1 tsp bicarbonate of soda

2 tbsp **honey** melted with **2 tbsp butter**

1 tbsp vegetable oil (for greasing)

Cornbread is also made using dried corn. You can use either cornmeal or polenta – the only difference is the consistency of the grain; polenta is finer than cornmeal. There are many dishes made using cornmeal – from baked goods to popular breakfast dishes in North America. You can make this in muffin cases, but a cast-iron skillet is the traditional way. Leftover cornbread is delicious made into a bread and butter pudding, or try it as French toast served with summer fruits – heavenly!

1. Preheat your oven to 180°C fan (350°F). Wipe the muffin tray, baking dish or cast-iron skillet with some oil, and place inside the oven.

2. Mix all the dry ingredients together in a bowl.

3. Stir the eggs and yoghurt together well, and then mix into the dry ingredients.

4. Pour the batter into your prepared baking receptacle carefully – you should hopefully hear a sizzle – then place in the oven.

5. Cook for 25 to 30 minutes if using a baking tray, 13 to 15 minutes for muffin cases. Insert a skewer into the middle and if it comes out clean, it's ready! If the cornbread is a little sticky, give it another couple of minutes in the oven.

6. Leave to cool, and then brush liberally with the honey and butter mixture before serving with fried chicken, barbecued ribs and coleslaw, chilli or stews.

CHALLENGE!
FERMENTING VEGETABLES

Making pickles and fermenting vegetables is one of the most nutritious ways to keep produce fresh for longer. Pickles can be found in almost every culture around the world; Korea is famous for its kimchi, while sauerkrauts are popular in Germany and Eastern Europe. Bread-and-butter pickles, and sweet pickles are enjoyed across America, and India has a wide range of pickled fruit.

TOP TIP
Always sterilise your jar before using it, and please wash your vegetables, hands and surfaces thoroughly before preparing.

There are two ways to pickle. One way is to use salt, which kills off the bad bacteria. Lactobacillus (*lak-tow-bah-si-luhs*) is the good bacteria that survives the salt, and gives the vegetables a sour taste. You can also quick-pickle by using vinegar.

Here is a method to start you off with your own lacto-fermented vegetables – all you need is salt, your chosen vegetable, a set of scales, a piece of muslin cloth and an airtight jar. It's best to use sea salt for this. Watch the fermentation process come alive as the days go by, observing the bubbles produced around the vegetable.

EXPERIMENT WITH FLAVOURS!

You could try:

Shredded carrot, white cabbage and caraway seeds

Fennel bulb, fresh ginger and cabbage

SauErKraut

1 small white cabbage, or half red and half white

1 ½ tbsp sea salt

This healthy recipe is packed full of probiotics, which is great for gut health. It's perfect added to sandwiches or served as a tasty side. Let's get pickling!

1. Remove any limp leaves from the cabbage and shred it by cutting into thin slices. Place in a large, clean bowl and sprinkle in the salt. Using clean hands, start scrunching and rubbing the cabbage together with the salt. This is fun, but make sure you check your hands for any cuts or scrapes beforehand, otherwise it will sting! Repeat for at least 10 minutes.

2. Pack the cabbage into your jar and press it down. Pour in any residual juice that has collected from the scrunching over the cabbage. Over the next day, keep pressing the cabbage down with the back of a spoon to release its juices. If you're having trouble keeping the cabbage submerged, a good tip is to fill a ziplock bag with water, seal and place on top of the cabbage to weigh it down, then replace the lid. Cover with a piece of muslin and a rubber band. If the cabbage hasn't released enough juice to cover itself after a day, dissolve a teaspoon of salt in 170ml (6fl. oz) of water, leave it to cool and add to the jar.

3. After 3 days, give it a taste. Keep tasting until you have your perfect tanginess, then store in the fridge!

All About Fish

The fish we eat can be categorised into two types – oily fish and white fish. Oily fish is rich in fatty acids and has many health benefits. It's often recommended to eat at least one portion of oily fish a week.

White fish is low in fat and high in protein, and also comes in two categories – round fish and flatfish. Round fish look just like ordinary fish, while flat fish are very thin, with eyes on the sides of their heads. They move sideways along the sea floor, just like a slippery carpet.

Monkfish

Coley

Pollock

ROUND FISH

Cod

Haddock

Sea bass

Hake

Skate

Turbot

FLATFISH

Plaice

Brill

Sole

Salmon

Trout

Whitebait

OILY FISH

Mackerel

Tuna

Anchovies

Eel

Herring

Kippers

Shrimp

Crayfish

Lobster

Cuttlefish

SHELLFISH

Oyster

Octopus

Crab

Scallop

Sea snail

DID YOU KNOW?

Although the word 'fish' is in their name, shellfish are not actually fish at all! Shellfish are species called molluscs or crustaceans. Most of these have hard exoskeletons (that means their skeletons are on the outside), or their soft bodies are housed inside shells. Squid, cuttlefish and octopuses are the exceptions. These creatures have 'beaks', a bit like birds.

Mussels

Clam

Winkle

How Many Ways Can

There are, as the saying goes, plenty of fish in the sea, but unfortunately there are not as many as there should be. Overfishing and the popularity of certain fish means that some species are now disappearing from the ocean, and need time to replenish. When you're buying fish, check where it has come from, and whether it is sustainable, which means it can be enjoyed responsibly.

Skin-on Cooking

As a very loose rule, any fish that has edible skin can be fried, grilled or roasted.

For sea bass, salmon, cod and mackerel, rub the skin with oil, and place in a cold, non-stick pan. Slowly bring up to a medium-high heat, while pressing down lightly with a spatula. This makes the skin go delightfully crisp.

Salmon fillets are perfect for poaching. It's important to keep the skin on while poaching and remove it carefully while the fish is cooling. Flabby fish skin isn't the most fun to eat.

For skate wings and thick pieces of cod, halibut or turbot, gently baste (by tilting the pan and spooning frequently) with butter.

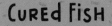

Cured Fish

Curing is a very old technique, and is often done by pickling or smoking the fish before eating. An easy way to cure fish at home is to make gravadlax:

1. Spread equal amounts of salt, sugar and dill over a piece of sushi-grade raw salmon.

2. Add another piece on top to make a sandwich and wrap the whole thing in clingfilm.

3. Place in the fridge and weigh down with a container.

4. Turn every day for 3 to 5 days and then brush off the 'cure' and serve in thin slices.

You Cook a Fish?

Almost any fish can be cooked in a variety of ways, though some methods are more suitable for certain fish than others. For example, battering and deep-frying a tuna steak wouldn't work as it's so meaty, and you may not consider haddock a good fish for sashimi. Trying as many varieties as possible will help you determine what cooking method works best.

Raw Fish

Fish that is uncooked can be just as delicious, but you need to make sure it is super fresh.

> **BIG PERSON TIP**
> *When buying fish, look for bright eyes, shiny skin and a mild seaside, – but not wrinkle-your-nose fishy – smell for ultimate freshness.*

Sushi Buying 'sushi-grade fish' means it's prepared with the highest hygiene standards. Eating raw fish that is not sushi-grade can make you very unwell. The Japanese have long been the experts when it comes to raw fish. It can take at least 10 years to learn to become a sushi pro, (known as an *itamae*). But don't let that put you off! Simple hand rolls with a variety of ingredients are a great place to start.

Poke (pronounced *poh-kay*) is a Hawaiian dish. Raw salmon and tuna are usually marinated in a variety of flavours. Salty, sour and spicy work really well for salmon, and salty with something sweet (such as honey), works fantastically with tuna.

Ceviche is a fantastic hit of summery freshness. Originally from South America, something acidic, such as lime juice, is used to lightly cure the fish before tumbling together with other ingredients such as onion, sweet potato and coriander.

CHINESE STEAMED FISH POUCHES

**SERVES 2 BIG PEOPLE
& 2 LITTLE PEOPLE**

4 firm, white skin-on fish fillets of even thickness

4 spring onions, topped, tailed and julienned into strips around a finger length

5cm (2in) piece of ginger, peeled and julienned

4 tsp light soy sauce

A pinch of sugar

3 tbsp mild-flavoured cooking oil

2 tbsp water

Aluminium foil

This method of steaming fish and then sizzling it with ginger and spring onion in oil, is Cantonese. It's very popular in Hong Kong and Southern China. The dramatic oil drizzle gives plenty of flavour, and firm white fish with skin, such as cod, bream, bass and hake, are best for this as they won't fall apart when cooked. The beauty of these delicious fish parcels is that they are quick but also super easy to make. The flavours are wonderfully simple, and allow the fish to shine.

1. Preheat the oven to 180°C (350°F). Lay the fillets skin-side down on a piece of foil on a baking tray. The foil needs to be big enough to fold over the fillets and pinch together into a roomy parcel.

2. Drizzle the water on and around the fish.

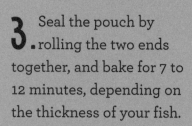

3. Seal the pouch by rolling the two ends together, and bake for 7 to 12 minutes, depending on the thickness of your fish.

4. When the fish is cooked, remove the parcel from the oven and open up the foil pouch carefully. Watch out for the steam! It will be very hot.

5. Lay the ginger and spring onion on top. Add a sprinkle of sugar, and a teaspoon of light soy sauce over each fillet.

6. Heat the cooking oil in a small saucepan until smoking. Then, very carefully, with the help of a Big Person, drizzle the oil on top of the ginger and spring onion and watch the drama unfold! This creates a wonderful aromatic smell, and also makes a delicious sauce to have on rice.

7. Serve the tray at the table, so everyone can pick their own pieces of fish. If you're cooking a whole fish instead of pieces, the cheek of the fish is the juiciest, and therefore the most prized morsel. Try not to fight over it!

OTHER pouch ideas:

These ideas involve cooking everything together at once. All you need is some rice, bread, potatoes or couscous to soak up the sauce.

Cod with olive oil, tomatoes, basil and capers.

Salmon with ginger, oyster sauce and tenderstem broccoli.

Haddock with thinly sliced fennel, butter and lemon.

Rainbow trout with spinach, dill and lemon.

Sea bream with olive oil, garlic, asparagus, cherry tomatoes and parsley.

Scallops with vermicelli noodles and black bean sauce.

Spiced Fish Fingers

MAKES 8 FISH FINGERS

300g fish fillet (cod, haddock, hake, pollock or salmon are great for this)

200g (~2 cups) plain flour

1 tsp ground coriander

½ tsp turmeric

1 tsp garam masala

A pinch of salt

1 tsp ground cumin

1 large egg, beaten

200g (~2 cups) panko breadcrumbs (or dry out some leftover bread in a warm oven and blitz in a blender)

Cooking spray or cooking oil

Fish fingers are so easy to pluck out of the freezer and cook, why would you make them yourself? Well, as much as frozen fish fingers are tasty, you can also use other types of fish to make fish fingers, and add different seasonings to the breadcrumb mix for a twist. Who knows, you may even prefer the ones you make yourself! There's something incredibly satisfying about a thick, chunky fish finger.

We're going to learn how to pané (pronounced *pan neigh* – like a horse!), and the key is to have one wet and one dry hand so you don't end up pané-ing your fingers! Pané simply means to coat something in seasoned flour, beaten egg and breadcrumbs before cooking.

1. Mix all the spices and salt together. Then, stir half of this into the flour and half into the breadcrumbs.

2. Lay out 3 bowls – one with the flour, one with the breadcrumbs and one with the beaten egg. At the end of the line, add a plate with a piece of greaseproof paper on top.

3. Preheat your oven to 170°C fan (325°F), and place a baking tray inside.

4. Slice the fish into strips that are around 3cm (1in) thick and as long as your Big Person's longest finger.

5. Using your dry hand, dip the fish strip into the flour and pat the flour around it. Then lift it out and shake off the excess. Next, place your floured fish finger into the egg. Using your wet hand, turn the fish to coat it, and then plop it into the breadcrumb bowl, trying not to touch the breadcrumbs.

BIG PERSON TIP
You can pop these straight into the freezer raw, but coated. Lay them on greaseproof paper so they don't stick together, and once frozen you can gather them up into a ziplock bag. Salmon can last up to 4 months in the freezer, and these fish fingers can be cooked straight from frozen.

6. Use your dry hand to pick up the crumbs and press them into the fish to coat it. Finally, lift up your breadcrumbed fish finger and place onto the greaseproof paper. Repeat with the remaining pieces.

7. Using the cooking spray, spritz your pre-heated baking tray well and place the fish fingers on it. Then spray the fish fingers too. You can also brush the tray with cooking oil. Bake for 12 to 14 minutes, but less if your fish fingers are thinner.

Challenge! The Cornershop

A corner shop is often a place to stop off and buy essentials, but you can also find a treasure trove of goods that will make a delicious meal. This challenge is all about tinned fish, which can sometimes be a little off-putting because of the pungent aroma when you first open it, but is actually delicious. Start with a couple of home comforts before you dive into something a little more adventurous. How many can you make?

Toast Toppers

Tinned fish is great spread on top of toast. Grill the bread on one side, then add the fish on the ungrilled side, and pop back under the grill for a couple of minutes. Anything in oil or brine should be drained first, and fish in sauces like tomato can be mashed in a bowl beforehand. Try adding spring or red onions, and cucumber or watercress, with a little lemon juice and a drizzle of olive oil to your topper.

Fishcakes

All you need for this dish is some tinned salmon or crab, leftover mash (potato, swede or celeriac), chopped herbs (dill or parsley work well), some flour, an egg, breadcrumbs and a dash of salt and pepper. Mix all the ingredients together, then roll a small handful into a ball and squish down slightly to make a patty. Pané (see page 46), spray with oil and bake or fry.

Noodle Soups

Curried noodle soups are perfect for tinned fish. Sizzle some curry paste in a little oil, loosen with coconut milk and simmer with tinned mackerel for a meal that packs a flavour punch. Slippery rice noodles are the best for this as they are light. Garnish with lime and a few coriander leaves, and if you're feeling especially hungry, add half a boiled egg.

Pasta Bake

won't win any awards, but this pasta bake is cheap and asy to make. All you need is some pasta (short shapes ork best), cheese (anything that melts), a tin of drained na, a tin of drained sweetcorn, a tin of cream of ushroom soup and some cornflour.

ok the pasta until it's almost done, then drain and d to a big bowl along with the tuna and sweetcorn. you happen to have an onion, chop that finely and row it in too. Then add the soup. Your mix should coated and a little saucy, but not drenched. nally, shake a teaspoon of cornflour over it and ix again. Pour into an oven dish, then top th cheese, and bake for 25 minutes at 160°C 20°F) fan, 180°C (350°F) without fan. The should be bubbling with crisp edges.

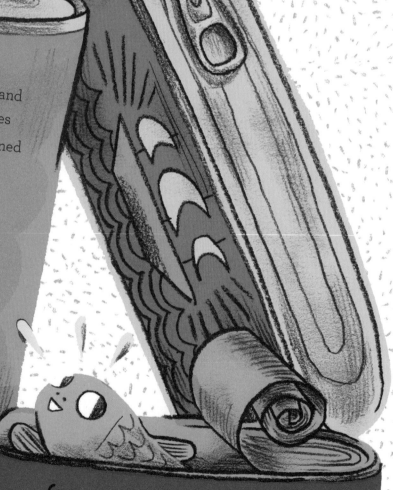

Creamy Salmon Crispbread

Mix some drained, tinned salmon with cream cheese, lemon juice, chives and pepper, then spread the mixture on crackers or crispbread for a quick snack.

FROM
THE
LAND

THE WORLD of MEAT

Animals were first domesticated for farming from about 13,000BCE.
Since then, the world's population has grown, and so has the
demand for meat, causing a big impact on the environment. Today,
we know a lot more about nutrition and how to balance our diets.
If you eat meat, look for sustainably reared and ethically farmed
products, which can help to decrease our carbon footprint.

Red Meat

Red meat is red when it's
raw, and dark-coloured once
cooked. Red meat includes
beef, lamb, mutton and pork.

Pork comes from pigs.
Rare-breed pigs are becoming
popular, especially fluffy
Mangalitzas. They have more
fat than traditional breeds
– and fat equals flavour.

Lamb is, to put it quite
simply, baby sheep. Meat
from older lambs is called
hogget, and meat from adult
sheep is called mutton.

Beef has many
classifications. In the US,
cows are often fed on grain,
but in the UK and Ireland,
they are generally grass-fed.
This affects the flavour.

POULTRY

Poultry comes from domesticated fowl, including chickens, ducks, turkeys and geese.

Chickens are the most popular poultry. We learn more about them on pages 54-55.

Glistening, bronzed **turkeys** are synonymous with Thanksgiving and Christmas celebrations.

Duck is also a fatty bird. The legs are best suited to long and slow cooking, while the breast can remain pink.

Geese are hard to source unless around Christmas time. They have a lot of fat and require careful cooking so that the meat doesn't dry out.

GAME

This refers to animals that are not domesticated and are hunted wild. Game animals include partridges, teals, grouse, quail and deer.

Most game is very lean, and requires careful cooking.

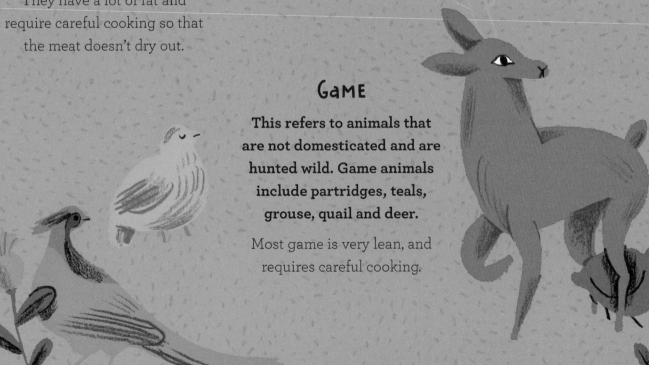

How Many Ways Can

Chicken is the most popular type of poultry in the world. In fact, there are over 20 billion chickens on Earth, easily outnumbering the human population! With its mild flavour and texture, chicken meat can be incorporated into a huge variety of meals and can be cooked in many ways.

There are lots of chicken breeds. If you're out shopping for chicken, free-range or organic meat is the best decision for flavour, chicken welfare and the impact on the environment.

Buying free-range or organic is more expensive, but a whole chicken can go a very long way, and this chapter will show you how. Every part of the chicken can, and should be, used for many delicious things.

If you are buying chicken that has already been cut into pieces, that's also OK! Interestingly, in different parts of the world, some parts of the chicken are more popular than in others. In the USA and Europe, the 'white' meat (the breasts), are highly prized, but in Asia and South America, 'dark' meat (the legs and thighs) is considered more desirable and flavoursome.

Whole Chicken

This can be roasted, barbecued or spatchcocked (split open and grilled). The whole chicken can also be chopped and stewed in popular dishes like coq au vin (braised with wine, vegetables and seasonings) and curries.

TOP TIP

Always wash your hands with warm, soapy water after handling raw chicken, and make sure to wash any surfaces or utensils you use too. Some chickens carry a bacteria that can make you ill if you digest it uncooked.

Legs and Thighs

These are fattier parts of the chicken with richer, more flavoursome meat. Because they are muscles (which are exercised more), they need a longer cooking time to become tender. Legs and thighs can be poached, roasted, barbecued, fried, or slow-cooked in stews or pies.

You Cook a Chicken?

Wings

The high ratio of skin to meat, and their size, means that wings are extremely flexible with how you cook them. High heat equals crisp skin, while cooking with sauce means they stay tender and juicy.

Breast

The breast is low in fat, but because of this it can also become overcooked very quickly. Overcooked chicken breast is dry and stringy – not a happy way to be! So while chicken must be cooked thoroughly, so no pink meat is seen, this is achieved quickly with chicken breasts. They can be used in quick-cook dishes, such as stir-fries and fried or breaded like schnitzels.

Carcass

You may not think that the chicken carcass has much appeal, but it makes a wonderful stock. This is a cooking liquid that can be used for soups, broths, stews or sauces to add flavour (see page 57).

DID YOU KNOW?

Silkie chickens have dramatically black bones, skin and organs. On the outside, they are covered in fluffy white feathers, making them look like walking fluffballs. In Chinese cuisine, especially Cantonese, silkie chickens are used for making soup – an exquisite, clear broth in particular, called 'double boiled'. It is highly prized for the skill needed to make it.

Brick Chicken

SERVES 2 BIG PEOPLE & 2 LITTLE PEOPLE

4 chicken thighs, de-boned with skin on

1 large piece of greaseproof paper

2 bricks (or a large frying pan and some heavy tins)

1 medium sized non-stick or cast-iron pan

1 tbsp cooking oil

Salt and pepper to taste

Things to do with brick chicken:

Pop in a burger bun, with mustard mayonnaise and shredded iceberg lettuce.

Drape in a feisty tomato, roasted pepper and paprika sauce.

Chop it up and throw it into a Caesar salad.

Drizzle with salsa verde – or any other green sauce (see page 26).

Pop it atop a creamy tarragon sauce.

Splat with harissa yoghurt and serve with jewelled couscous.

Brick chicken is so called because it uses a brick as a weight to press the chicken down. If you don't have one lying around, you can use a frying pan loaded with heavy tins. Anything weighty will do! Brick chicken is the absolute best way to cook chicken simply, so that you have juicy insides and crispy outsides. This style of chicken is so flexible that you can use it in many different ways. Let's get sizzling!

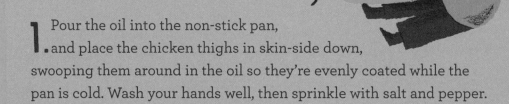

1. Pour the oil into the non-stick pan, and place the chicken thighs in skin-side down, swooping them around in the oil so they're evenly coated while the pan is cold. Wash your hands well, then sprinkle with salt and pepper.

2. Place the greaseproof paper on top of the chicken thighs, then place your brick or weighted frying pan on top.

3. Turn on the heat, and allow the pan to heat up slooooooowly. When you hear it start to sizzle, keep the heat at a medium setting. Ask a Big Person to check the chicken for a deep golden-brown on the outside, using a pair of tongs. This will take about 15 minutes.

4. When the skin turns a rich toffee colour, ask a Big Person to flip the thighs over, lay the greaseproof paper back on top and cook for another minute. Make sure to stand back, as the hot oil can spit!

Phở Gà

**SERVES 2 BIG PEOPLE
& 2 LITTLE PEOPLE**

A chicken carcass

500g chicken thighs or breasts

Half an onion, with skin on

A knob of ginger, skin on, sliced
  into long, thick long pieces

A few garlic cloves

2 star anise

2 cloves

1 tsp fennel seeds

1 tsp coriander seeds

1 cinnamon stick

Flat rice noodles

A splash of fish sauce

A dash of sugar

1 lime

Coriander, Thai basil
  and beansprouts,
  to serve

Once you've roasted a chicken and made use of all, if not most, of it, make sure you save the carcass. It may not look tasty, but it makes a delicious base for many dishes. For example, you could use it to make this famous Vietnamese noodle soup: Phở Gà. 'Phở' refers to the style of noodle that's used for this soup – a flat rice noodle that's sold dried. Phở Gà is truly one of the most comforting, satisfying meals around. Many eat it for breakfast in Vietnam, but it's perfect any time of the day.

1. Using a pair of tongs, scorch the onion, garlic and ginger under a hot grill, turning frequently until they catch at the sides. Ask a Big Person to help you with this.

2. Sling these into the pot with the chicken carcass, skin and all.

3. Add 2 star anise, 2 cloves, fennel seeds, coriander seeds and a stick of cinnamon.

4. Add enough water to cover the chicken, then place on the heat and bring it to just below the boil. Once you see bubbles breaking the surface, turn the heat right down, pop the lid on and leave it. For *hours*. Get some homework done, watch a film – whatever you like! After 3 hours, you will have broth that looks like liquid gold.

5. Leave it to cool, then when you're ready (with the help of a Big Person), strain the bones and spices out. You now have your noodle soup stock.

6. To make Phở Gà, chop some chicken breasts or thighs and poach them in the broth.

7. In a bowl, add some cooked noodles and season with fish sauce, sugar and lime juice.

8. Bring the broth to a hearty simmer and then ladle on top of the noodles. Serve with the herbs for everyone to add at will.

CHICKEN CURRY

SERVES 2 BIG PEOPLE AND 2 LITTLE PEOPLE

2 chicken breasts (around 300g/10oz each)

1 large white onion, diced finely

3 garlic cloves, minced

5cm (2in) piece of ginger, peeled and minced

1 green chilli (if you're brave!), sliced into rings

1 tin of whole plum tomatoes

200ml (~7fl. oz.) coconut cream

1 tbsp tomato puree

1 tbsp cumin seeds

2 tbsp ground coriander

2 tsp turmeric

½ tsp ground cinnamon

A few pinches of salt

1 tbsp garam masala

1 tbsp cooking oil

1 tbsp butter

A handful of coriander leaves

Rice of your choosing

Zingy, spicy, tasty! A chicken curry can be rich, luxurious and flavoursome even with a short cooking time. Many recipes use chicken with the bones in, which can be fiddly to eat – especially once covered in sauce! In this recipe, we use chicken breasts and a lot of spices. Each one has its own distinctive flavour, so be sure to give them a good sniff before you throw them in.

1. First, marinate the chicken. Chop the chicken breasts up into even, bite-sized pieces, then mix the turmeric and coconut cream together. Turn the chicken pieces to coat them in the marinade. You can do this any time up to 24 hours before you start cooking.

2. In a large frying pan, add the cooking oil and place on a medium heat. When shimmering, add the onions and cumin seeds, and fry very slowly, for about 15 minutes, until they turn a deep bronze – but not burnt!

3. Add the ginger, garlic and chilli (if you're using it), and turn them around the pan a few times until it smells fragrant and delicious.

4. Next, add the ground coriander, cinnamon and butter, and let them sizzle for a couple of minutes, stirring all the while. Breathe in those aromas!

5. In a large bowl, tip out the tomatoes. Then get your hands in there and squidge! Squash them until they're all broken up, then add to the frying pan with the tomato puree, stirring well. Add the salt here, too. Let this mixture simmer for 10 to 15 minutes, until you have a dry-ish masala (that's the word for a spiced gravy), but not so much that it sticks to the bottom of the pan.

6. Add the marinated chicken to the masala and turn it around in the sauce so that everything is evenly mixed together.

7. Now is a good time to get the rice on. Cook according to the packet's instructions.

8. Back to the curry! Stir in the garam masala, and then cook on a low simmer, stirring 2 or 3 times, for 12 to 15 minutes, until the chicken pieces are cooked through.

9. Garnish with coriander and serve with the rice. Cucumber and tomato salad with a slice of lemon on the side is also a great accompaniment.

Challenge!
Meat on Sticks

Wherever you go in the world, you'll find some sort of meat on sticks. From kebabs to satay, the difference lies in spicing, flavourings and the meat itself, while the cooking format largely remains the same – hot flames gently flavouring the meat with smoke. The meat can be marinated, rubbed with spices or even brushed with sauce afterwards – and often a combination of all three. It's so exciting that just a change of herb or spice on a common protein can transport you to a different country entirely. How many of these delicious dishes can you make?

Suya (Western Africa)

Beef, mutton or chicken is marinated in a complex mix of spices called *yaji*, and served with a spice mix for dipping after it's cooked, too.

Yakitori (Japan)

Various parts of the chicken are grilled and glazed with *tare* (made with soy sauce, mirin, sake and sugar).

Satay (Southeast Asia)

Chicken, pork, mutton or beef (each country has a different recipe for satay) is marinated with flavours including lemongrass, sugar, garlic, coriander, cumin, turmeric, galangal and shallots.

Moo Ping (Thailand)

Pork is marinated in garlic, fish sauce, sugar, peppercorns and coconut milk.

Sosaties
(South Africa)

Chicken, lamb or mutton are marinated in sweet chilli sauce, with lemon and herbs, or fried onions, chillies, garlic, curry leaves and tamarind juice. The meat is often threaded with dried apricots or prunes on a skewer.

Xinjiang Skewers
(China)

These are often made with lamb pieces interspersed with fat, or kidneys, but can also be made with fish. Chilli powder, cumin, salt and Sichuan peppercorns are included in the spice mix.

TOP TIP

If you're using wooden skewers, it's a good idea to soak them in cold water for a couple of hours first to stop them from burning; otherwise, metal skewers are great - just be sure to use oven gloves to protect you from the hot end.

Adana
(Turkey)

Minced lamb is mixed with chilli flakes, garlic, parsley, cinnamon, fennel, fenugreek, cumin and coriander seeds.

Grillfackeln
(Germany)

Romantically named 'barbecue torches', these skewers are made with pork belly, curry powder, garlic and paprika, served with fried onion and a sour cream dip.

Souvlaki
(Greece)

These skewers are made from chicken or pork with garlic, oregano, lemon, olive oil and sweet paprika.

EGGS AND DAIRY

All About Dairy...

'Dairy' is the name we use for any produce containing milk from a mammal. Lots of animals produce milk. We normally think of cows, goats and sheep, but horse, reindeer and even camel milk is consumed by people around the world! Depending on the animal and the amount of fat, animal milk can be used to make dairy products including yoghurt, cheese and butter.

Cream
(thick milk)

Cheese
(aged milk)

Kefir
(a fermented milk drink)

Buttermilk
(a by-product of butter)

Butter
(the fat of milk)

Yoghurt
(thick, fermented milk)

How to make butter

To make butter, you just need cream and lots of agitation (stirring and shaking) – all you are doing is separating fat from milk. You'll also need a jar with a tight-fitting lid, and a lot of energy! Start by shaking 500ml (~17fl. oz.) double cream. Keep going until the fat has separated from the milk (and your arms may have fallen off!). The liquid left behind is called buttermilk. Pour the buttermilk in a separate bowl, then scoop the fat into a ball and place in a large metal bowl. Bunch it together and squeeze, then pour iced water over it, and repeat the process. Keep rinsing and squishing until the water runs clear. Now you have butter!

...and Eggs!

Eggs are laid by lots of different animals, including fish, reptiles and birds. From pearl-sized caviar to ostrich eggs as big as balloons, there is a huge variety that have been farmed for human consumption. In this chapter, we take a deep dive into how wonderfully useful eggs are.

Caviar is from sturgeon (a type of fish), and of all the eggs, it is the most expensive.

Roe is often eaten raw or salted. Some types are popular with sushi.

Fish roe

Chicken

Quail

Turkey

Caviar

Dainty quails eggs are best peeled by those with small and dexterous fingers!

Versatile hen eggs can be used in so many ways (see pages 66-67).

Turkey eggs are fairly rare, mainly because turkeys only lay two per week. Hens lay three times that amount.

Goose

Goose eggs are so large, they could cover your entire hand!

Duck

Ostrich

Duck eggs have a lovely pale-blue shell.

Emu

You might be hard-pressed to find an emu egg, but if you do you'll be wowed by its blue-green colour.

Ostrich eggs are the largest on Earth! They are also the toughest. With a shell a couple of millimetres thick, you might need a power drill to open it up!

How Many Ways Can

Eggs are MAGIC! Their uses are endless, whether in sweet or savoury cooking. Whole eggs, egg whites and egg yolks all have different properties, but because they have so many, you should never throw any part of an egg away! Egg whites freeze really well, and egg yolks can be kept in the fridge for two days, covered with water to stay moist.

Egg Whites

Also known as 'albumen', this is the mega airy binding ingredient.

You can use egg whites to make meringue, pavlova, macaroons and macarons, mousse, soufflé, marshmallow, icing, sorbet, semifreddo (a semi-frozen Italian dessert), or for marinating meat, also known as 'velveting' (a Chinese method). Phew!

Egg Yolks

Yolks can be made into custard, carbonara, pasta dough, citrus curd, enriched bread dough and sauces such as Béarnaise, hollandaise and mayonnaise. They can also be cooked and grated, or cured.

Egg Shells

Egg shells make excellent bird feed. Wash and bake the shells at 120°C fan (248°F) until dried and brittle. Crush them up and leave them out for the birds.

TOP TIP

One egg always has a stronger shell than the other. So, the best way of cracking an egg is to lightly tap one against the other: only one will break.

You Cook an Egg?

One of the main things to know about eggs is that they are very delicate! If they are dropped, knocked or squeezed they will break, so you should handle them very gently. Interestingly, eggs have less chance of breaking if you drop them on their pointy end – in fact, egg drops without breaking are something of a cult hobby! Egg-spert David Donoghue dropped an egg out of a helicopter onto a golf course without it breaking in 1994. I don't recommend you try to recreate this! Whole eggs can be used in all sorts of ways:

Egg drop soup

Frittata

Avgolemono
(Greek chicken soup with lemon, thickened with egg)

Pickled

Tortilla

Fried

Scrambled

Soft-boiled

Omelette

Poached

Cake

Pastry

MENEMEN

SERVES 2 BIG PEOPLE
& 1 LITTLE PERSON

5 eggs

1 tbsp olive oil

2 large, ripe tomatoes, diced

2 long, green, pointed
Turkish peppers or
1 green bell pepper

1 small onion, peeled
and diced

A pinch of chilli
flakes (optional)

1 tsp sweet paprika

1 tsp ground cumin

A large pinch of dried thyme

A similarly large pinch
of dried oregano

A pinch of salt

A small handful of
chopped flat parsley

This traditional dish comes from Turkey and while it might
not look the most appealing, it tastes of sunshine and
spice. Not only is menemen fun to say, it's also perfect for
a weekend breakfast with a buttered baguette. *Menemen*
is best made in the height of summer, when tomatoes are
ripe and juicy and almost bursting from their skins.

1. Warm the oil in a medium frying pan. Fry the
onion gently for around 5 minutes, until soft.

2. Add the green pepper and cook until
softened, then add the chilli (if using),
paprika, cumin, dried thyme, oregano and salt.

3. Stir to combine, then add the tomatoes
and cook on a medium heat for around 5
minutes, stirring occasionally. You're looking
for some of the tomato juice to evaporate, but
not so much that the tomato catches or sticks.

4. Take the pan off the heat, and crack the
eggs directly into it. Then return the pan
to a low heat and mix everything well.

5. Stir slowly. Allow the eggs to begin to
set, and then stir again. Do this until the
eggs are creamy, but not solid or powdery.

6. Top with parsley. Dip your bread in Turkish
-style and pile the menemen on top!

Custard

300ml (~11fl. oz.) whole milk

200ml (~7fl. oz.) double cream

55g (~¼ cup) caster sugar

1 tsp vanilla bean paste or ½ vanilla bean pod

3 egg yolks from large eggs

TOP TIP
Adding sugar to the milk and cream mixture will prevent a burnt skin forming on the bottom of your pan.

Making your own custard is a wonderful way to observe the science behind cooking eggs. You mustn't leave your custard alone for the merest of seconds – if you take your eye off it, or if you stop whisking, you may end up with gooey, milky scrambled eggs. Not great for your crumble! But once you master custard (and you will!) not only will your winter comfort desserts be transformed, but you also have a base for great ice cream. Let's get stirring...

1. Add the milk and cream to a medium-sized saucepan. Next add half the sugar and warm on a medium heat.

2. Add the remaining sugar to a mixing bowl and then add the yolks. Start whisking energetically and immediately! Whisk until the sugar has dissolved.

3. You might need a helping hand with this next bit. When the milk mixture is steaming and almost boiling (you will see little bubbles start to break), pour half the mixture over the eggs and whisk like crazy so that the eggs don't set.

4. Add the egg mixture back to the pan, and swap to a wooden spoon. Stir slowly and continuously, while the mixture heats up again. This can take a while, so don't rush. You want it to get to 80°C (192°F), so use a cooking thermometer to get the right temperature.

5. Remove from the heat, pour into a jug, and either use immediately or leave to cool and cover with cling film. Place the jug in a pan of hot water and stir well with a spoon to re-heat. Do this slowly to prevent the custard from over-cooking.

ANOTHER TIP
You can also judge yourself when it's ready – when the custard gets thick enough to draw a line with the back of a wooden spoon and it leaves a trail, it's done.

69

QUICHE

SERVES 4 BIG PEOPLE

1 sheet of ready-made
  shortcrust pastry

Three eggs

175ml (~6fl. oz.) whole milk

125ml (~4fl. oz.) double cream

A 25cm (10in) pastry tin

A filling of your choice

A pinch of salt and pepper

A LESSON IN VOLUME

Volume is very important
to a well-filled quiche. The
general rule is one part egg
to two parts of liquid dairy
(in volume, not weight).
The liquid dairy should be
half double cream and half
whole milk. It's important
to measure the ingredients,
and here is a tip to help
you. Crack your egg over a
bowl. Hopefully your egg
shell should have split fairly
evenly. Now, mix your milk
and cream together. Start
with 250ml in a measuring
jug. Pour the milk/cream mix
up to the brim of your egg
shell halves. Place in the bowl
with the egg. Then you have
an egg-to-dairy volume ratio
of 1:1. Scoop and pour the
liquid again for the second
part. Repeat this process
for three eggs for a 25cm
(10in) loose-bottomed case.

'Quiche' is a French word, which originates from the German *kuchen*,
which means cake. Quite simply a quiche is an egg cake – a savoury
custard surrounded by shortcrust pastry. If you can get the consistency
right so that it is light yet rich, silky and smooth, you will have a
very versatile recipe up your sleeve that you can add to. Asparagus
season? Quiche! Time for a picnic? Quiche! Cooking lunch for the
grandparents? Quiche! Leftover Christmas ham? Quiche Lorraine!

1. Preheat your oven to 160°C fan (320°F).

2. Roll out the shortcrust pastry evenly to around 2cm (0.8in)
thick and place into your case so it hangs over the sides.

3. Bring the edge of the pastry vertically against the rim and
push down so that it's tucked in, then drape over the side. Do
this all the way round. Trim the excess, but make sure you have a
little bit of overhang – the pastry will shrink when it's cooked.

Quiche filling ideas:

For quiche fillings, anything you want to add should be pre-cooked.
Some vegetables can be placed on top while raw, though, like asparagus spears.
Here are some lovely flavour combinations to try. Cheese is always a
good idea, regardless of anything else you want to add!

**Onion, bacon, thyme and cheddar
(a classic quiche Lorraine).**

Tomato, basil and roasted red pepper.

Mushroom and tarragon.

**Smoked salmon, soft, garlicky
cheese and asparagus.**

Sweet potato, feta and caramelised onion.

Goats cheese and red onion.

4. Line with greaseproof paper and fill with baking beans or rice. This will keep the base flat.

5. Bake at 160°C (320°F) in a fan oven for 12–18 minutes. Keep peeking and when it's lightly golden-brown, remove from the oven.

6. Leave to cool on the side before lifting the weights out. Next, spread your cooked filling around the base, place your pastry case back on the oven shelf, and very carefully, pour your custard into it. It's important to do it this way round, as lowering or lifting a case full of liquid into the oven is very tricky! As carefully as you can, slide the shelf back into the oven and shut the door.

7. Bake for 40 minutes, until you have a slight wobble in the middle of the quiche when you give it a light jiggle.

8. Remove your quiche from the oven and leave on the side to cool completely before removing it from the case. This is best done by placing the bottom evenly on top of an upside-down bowl and sliding the case edge down, then using a spatula to remove from the base. Completely cooled, of course!

Challenge!
Ultimate Cheesy Toastie

Before you get stuck into this stringy, gloopy, super cheesy chart, let's first look at how to make a cheese toastie. Bread. Cheese. Toasted together with some kind of heat. That's it!

But to make the ultimate delicious cheese toastie, you could also think about adding pickles and chutneys. These tangy vegetables cut through the richness of the cheese beautifully. If you had a go at making your own pickled vegetables on pages 36–37, why not add them in here? You don't need a specialist machine to make these. A non-stick frying pan, greaseproof paper and a saucepan weighted with tin cans to press the toastie down is all you need!

BREAD

CHEESE

Swiss

Red Leicester

Gouda

Jarlsberg

Gruyère

Cheddar

Camembert

Fontina

Mozzarella

Brie

VEGETABLES

Sliced tomato

Spring onion

Artichoke

Red onion

Baby leaf spinach

Roasted red pepper
(jarred or home-made)

PICKLES AND CHUTNEYS

Sauerkraut

Quince jelly

Branston's pickle

Fig jam

Piccalilli

EXTRAS

Mustard

Pastrami

Cabbage kimchi

Roast beef

Deli meats

Baked beans

BREAD

TOP TIP

Whatever combination you decide to make, buttering the outside of the bread with mayonnaise before toasting will give you a beautifully burnished crust.

PASTA,
AND DU

NOODLES
MPLINGS

The World of Pasta and Noodles

What came first, pasta or noodles? While China and Italy fight to claim the title, there's no clear winner. A 4,000-year-old bowl of noodles was discovered in Lajia in northwestern China, however, making it the earliest evidence of noodles ever found. But were these noodles the ancestor of Asian noodles or Italian pasta? We just don't know . . .

Capellini

Penne

Fusilli

Orzo

Linguine

PASTA

This is by no means a list of every pasta in existence – that would be a book in itself – but some of the more commonly found shapes. Each shape has a sauce it is ideal for; short shapes and tubes are well suited to hearty, meaty sauces, while noodle-like shapes are great for slurping up smooth sauces.

Casarecce

Spaghetti

Orecchiette

Garganelli

Mafaldine

Pappardelle

Conchiglie

Paccheri

Tagliatelle

Bucatini

Trofie

Farfalle

Rigatoni

Macaroni

Rice

Rice noodles are often used to make soups, such as the Vietnamese dish **Phở Gà** (see page 57).

Buckwheat

Soba noodles hail from Japan. They are naturally gluten-free as they are made from 100% buckwheat flour.

Wheat

Jjolmyeon noodles are thick and chewy, and can be eaten cold.

Egg and Alkaline

Not all egg noodles have egg in them; some Chinese noodles are called egg noodles simply because they are egg-yellow in colour, made using alkaline ingredients to make them chewier.

Starch

Cellophane, or glass, noodles are made using mung bean, potato, sweet potato or tapioca starch.

NOODLES

The humble noodle can be defined as any long strand shape, made of virtually any starch, and cooked by boiling, frying, deep frying or steaming. The type of starch used and the sauce they're cooked with, defines whether it is pasta or noodle. Indeed, in the US people call pasta shaped like spaghetti . . . noodles!

All About Dumplings

There is a vast array of dumplings from all around the world. Xiao Long Bao are a famous magical dumpling from China that are steamed and have soup inside them – amazing! From Jewish households feasting on kreplach for their traditional Friday night dinners, to Ukrainians celebrating summer with sour cherry *vareniki*, you can be sure that someone, somewhere is eating a dumpling at any given moment.

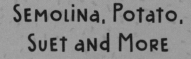
English dumplings

Tortelloni

Ravioli

Semolina, Potato, Suet and More

Roll, stuff and go! These could perhaps be known as the starter -level of dumplings, given the forgiving nature of the dough.

Pastas

A little more elbow grease is required to get the dough nice and thin – definitely one to set aside a Sunday for, as these dumplings (like ravioli) can take a while!

Wonton

Tang Yuan
(*brightly coloured desert balls*)

Coxinha

Gomari
(*look like fish!*)

Jamaican Fried Dumplings

WHEAT DOUGH DUMPLINGS

Quite simply, these are made from flour and water, kneaded, rolled and folded. Sometimes fat or salt is added, sometimes not.

RICE AND TAPIOCA STARCH DUMPLINGS

These dumplings are tricky and fiddly. The water ratio must be just right, and they are prone to tearing due to the lack of gluten. These are ones to save for when you become a dumpling-making pro.

One-Pot Pasta

SERVES 2 BIG PEOPLE AND 1 LITTLE PERSON

300g (~11oz) dried spaghetti

250g (~9oz) cherry tomatoes, halved

1 courgette, top and tail removed, cut lengthways twice and then chopped 3cm (~1in) thick (so each cut makes 6 pieces)

Zest of 1 lemon

3 cloves of garlic, peeled and minced

1 tsp salt

A glug of olive oil

1 ½ tbsp mascarpone or cream cheese

A handful of basil leaves

Parmesan, to serve

This spaghetti recipe is a real saviour if you want something filling and luxurious . . . and you've left the kitchen in a mess one too many times! It's time to get back into the Big People's good books. All you need (to wash up later) is a frying pan large enough to fit spaghetti in without having to break it, a chopping board, a knife and a kettle . . . and of course, the dishes you've already eaten off of!

1. Arrange the dried spaghetti in the centre of the frying pan. Add the courgettes and tomatoes either side of it. Throw the lemon zest on top and then add the salt and the garlic.

2. Glug the olive oil with some Italian flair! (Imagine you're a chef in a Tuscan villa).

3. Ask a Big Person to boil 750ml (~26 fl. oz.) of water in a kettle, and carefully pour it over your pasta. Bring it to the boil on the highest heat, and then turn down to medium – you want to achieve a lively simmer.

4. Using a pair of tongs, every 30 seconds to a minute, toss, toss, toss.

5. Keep tossing! Around 6 or 7 minutes later, your pasta should be perfectly cooked.

6. Turn the heat down to low, and add the mascarpone or cream cheese so it melts. Then stir in half the basil.

7. Serve! Raise the tongs high in the air with the pasta and place carefully onto the plate. Follow with all the delicious pieces of courgette and sauce. Garnish with the rest of the basil and a flurry of parmesan and black pepper.

Sesame Peanut Noodles

**SERVES 1 BIG PERSON
& 1 LITTLE PERSON**

200g (~7oz) dried noodles

1 tbsp roasted sesame oil

1 large clove of garlic, minced

2 tbsp sesame paste

2 tbsp chunky or smooth
  peanut butter

1 tbsp hot water

1 tbsp light soy sauce

½ tbsp of Chinese black
  or balsamic vinegar

½ cucumber, peeled
  and julienned

1 carrot, peeled and julienned

A handful of any kind of
  crunchy greens (such as
  cabbage), finely sliced

1 spring onion, finely sliced

These sesame peanut noodles are incredibly quick, but are delicious and filling. Perfect for summertime lunches, a quick dinner or to pack up for a picnic, these noodles are also a great way to use up odds and ends. You're looking for crunch to contrast with the soft, silky noodles. Any wheat or egg noodles cooked from dried work wonderfully here. If you can't find Chinese noodles, try linguine.

1. Cook the dried noodles in plenty of water as per the packet instructions. Drain, then toss with the roasted sesame oil so that the noodles don't stick together.

2. Mix the sesame paste and peanut butter with the light soy sauce, vinegar and garlic. It might be quite stiff to mix, so stir in the hot water to help. Add more to get a smoother consistency if needed. In a large bowl, dress the noodles with this sauce.

TOP TIP
*Keep your tahini or sesame paste
in the fridge, otherwise the paste
and the oil separates and it's a lot
of elbow grease to reincorporate it.*

3. When the noodles have cooled, add the vegetables and serve!

Beijing-Style Dumplings with Dipping Sauce

MAKES 24–30 DUMPLINGS

For the dough:

250g (2 ½ cups) plain flour

130ml (~5fl. oz.) water

These dumplings are super easy to make, but need a bit of practise to perfect the technique. Have fun with the dough – you don't have to do any complicated folding, but it's important that the dumplings are sealed well. Spend a rainy afternoon indoors perfecting them, and in no time at all you'll be able to mix up a batch using flavours to suit your mood and the seasons.

1. Using chopsticks or a spatula, gradually mix the water into the flour until there is no loose flour left. Use your hands to squeeze and push the mixture into a ball. Cover the bowl with a tea towel for 15 minutes to let the gluten relax.

2. Knead the dough until it's looking smooth, place back in the bowl and cover with the cloth again – this time for 1 hour.

3. The dough should now be, as the Chinese say, 'as soft as an earlobe'. Roll it into a long sausage, about as thick as a broom handle. Measure out 4 equal lengths, and leave 3 under the cloth while you work on one. Cut into 6 equal pieces. On a lightly floured surface, squash a piece with your hand and then roll into a circle using a small rolling pin.

For the filling:

200g (1 cup) pork mince (at least 20% fat)

3 spring onions, minced

1 tsp minced ginger, submerged in 1 tbsp water

A large pinch of salt

1 tsp light soy

½ tsp sesame oil

1 tsp oyster sauce

1. Mix all your ingredients together with a fork or chopsticks.

2. Stir well until it has all combined.

3. Refrigerate until ready to use.

BIG PERSON TIP
Ask your butcher to mince you 60% pork shoulder with 40% pork belly, if you can.

4. Now you have your dumpling wrapper! Add a heaped teaspoon of filling to the centre while it's sat on your palm. Bring the edges up together, and squeeze to seal.

5. To cook, place the dumpling on a ladle, and one by one, lower them into a large pot of simmering water, and cook for 4–5 minutes. Use the ladle to fish them out, place into a colander or sieve, and drain well.

For the dipping sauce:

1 tbsp light soy sauce

3cm (1in) ginger, peeled and julienned

1 tbsp Chinese black vinegar (substitute with 1 tsp red wine vinegar + 1 tsp balsamic vinegar if necessary)

½ tsp sugar

Chilli oil (optional)

1. Mix all of the ingredients and serve with the dumplings to dip into.

CHALLENGE!
MAKING NOODLES

300g (1 ¾ cup) strong white bread flour (needed for the high gluten content – look at the back of the flour packet for a 'protein' listing between 11 and 14%)

¼ tsp salt

153g water (5 ½ fl. oz.) (weighing water is quicker than using a measuring jug!)

Making your own noodles at home can seem like a challenge, but all you really need is flour, water, patience and some elbow grease. The beauty of noodles is that they don't need to be perfect – we want the noodles to be a bit craggy! Noodles with ridges and tears catch the sauce more easily.

1. In a large bowl, add the flour and the salt. Pour in half the water and mix with a wooden spoon. It will look quite dry and shaggy.

2. Add the rest of the water and continue to mix. Combine with your hands, pressing everything together to form a ball. It will still look dry, but resist the temptation to add more water.

3. Turn out onto a surface and knead by pushing the dough together, turning and repeating. You'll have to do this for 15 minutes. Put on some tunes, have a dance, and maybe even swap with someone to give yourself a rest!

LET'S TALK ABOUT GLUTEN...

Gluten is a protein that is found in flour; it makes things chewy and springy. For delicate, crumbly cakes, we don't want any gluten at all, so, when we use flour to make a cake, we stir it briefly to make a batter, then we leave it alone. But for noodles, we need them to be robust – so they are able to be pulled, stirred and slurped. Kneading the dough activates the gluten; it gets the dough excited and it forms bonds so that becomes strong. But we also need the gluten to relax a bit, to help with texture and for the dough to absorb the water fully. That's why we excite it, then rest it.

4. At this point, you will have a tight dough ball. Be warned: it won't look very pretty. Leave on the counter top, cover with the bowl you mixed it in and leave to rest for 45 minutes.

5. Give the ball another 5 minutes of kneading, cover and then rest for another 30 minutes.

6. Cut the ball in half and keep one half covered. With a large rolling pin, roll the sheet out to 2mm (1/16 in) thickness. The dough will keep springing back towards you – which means the gluten is nicely developed – but persevere with it.

7. Flour the top of the sheet well, and fold it up lengthways 4 times into a wide rectangle. Use a sharp knife and cut it lengthways into strips, around 1mm (1/32 in) in width.

8. Tumble your new noodles with your fingers, prising the strips apart to separate them.

9. Cook in boiling water for 1–3 minutes, depending on their thickness, then drain.

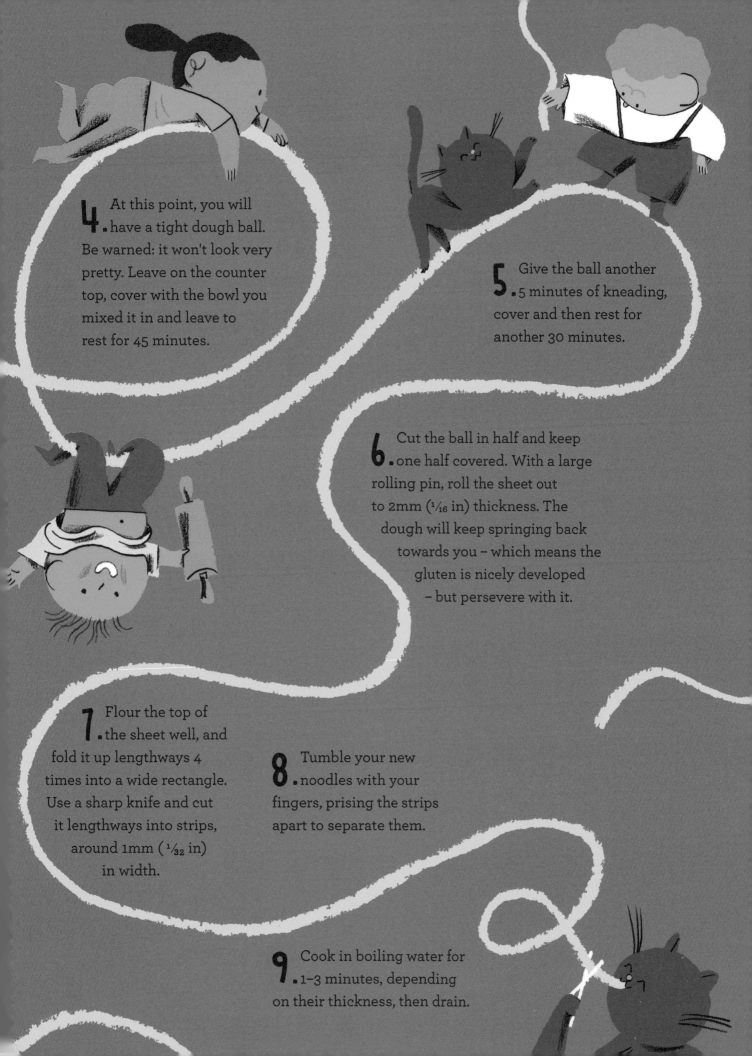

The World of Grains

Cereals and grains make up the bulk of most peoples' diets,
so to say that they are important would be a big understatement!

Bran

Endosperm

Germ

Grains are made up of three sections: the bran, which is the outermost layer, and full of fibre and B vitamins; the germ (not to be confused with germs like bacteria!), which is also called the 'embryo' and contains oils and vitamins; and the endosperm, which sits above the embryo, and contains the protein and carbohydrate.

Rye

Rye is popular in bread-making because it adds a nutty flavour. Rye bread is well-liked in Nordic countries.

Buckwheat

This small nutty seed is usually ground into flour to make savoury crepes and soba noodles. It's eaten as a whole grain, simply steamed and buttered, across Russia (called *kasha*).

Oats

The unofficial national dish of Scotland, porridge is made using oats, which is one of the few grains that grows well in the rugged countryside. Steel-cut, rolled or instant – oats are always used whole.

Bulgur

Bulgur is a tiny grain made from dried kernels of wheat. Cooked by steaming, bulgur is eaten all over the Middle East, and is an essential ingredient in tabbouleh, a fragrant salad made up mostly of parsley.

Farro

An Italian grain, farro is mainly grown in the central and northern regions, and is often used in salads.

Millet

Millet can be yellow, grey, white or red, and is eaten widely across India and China as porridge, or ground into flour to make roti (Indian bread).

Teff

Teff is a type of millet and is a staple grain in Ethiopia. It is fermented, then ground to make injera – a spongy flatbread eaten with curries.

Quinoa

A Peruvian grain more than 5,000 years old, quinoa (pronounced *keen-wah*) is considered a 'complete protein' and is often served as salad or with rice.

Wheat

One of the most widely grown crops, wheat is used to make bread, noodles, pasta, cakes, cookies and muffins – almost every country in the world has a use for wheat.

Barley

Great for soups and stews, barley has a nutty flavour and a slippery feeling in the mouth.

All About Rice

Rice is a staple food for millions of people all over the world, and is so widely loved that it's grown on three different continents! Currently, China is the biggest consumer, followed by India, Indonesia, Bangladesh, Vietnam, the Philippines and Thailand. The first non-Asian country to hit this list, in at number 10, is Brazil.

Rice can be categorised easily by the size of the grain: long or short. It also comes as a whole grain, with the husks still attached (known as brown rice), or polished white grains.

Wild rice

Wild rice grains are long, and are often found mixed with other rice. This rice is much chewier than it's white counterparts, and is often used in salads.

Jasmine rice

Long-Grain Rice

Most commonly eaten in India, basmati rice is distinctively fragrant and certainly what you would be served with an Indian meal.

Mostly grown in Thailand, jasmine rice has a different perfume when cooked.

Broken rice

Usually found in cheaper Asian supermarkets, broken rice is budget-friendly rice that is, literally, all the broken grains that don't go into the more expensive bags. Perfect for making rice porridge!

These varieties are used for paella, and they absorb a lot of moisture without becoming sticky.

Calasparra and Bomba rice

Sushi rice is preferred in Japan. It is sticky when cooked and retains shape easily.

Sushi rice

This rice is incredibly sticky – more so than sushi rice – and is often used in sweet dessert dishes, or in Thailand, served alongside salads.

Black sticky rice

This is the wholegrain version of sticky rice, and has a dramatic purple hue when cooked. It is also used mainly for desserts, and sweet soups or drinks in Asia.

Sticky rice

SHORT-GRAIN RICE

Arborio and carnaroli – most commonly found in Italy – are perfect for risottos, and need slow cooking to coax out their starchy creaminess.

TOP TIP

All of these different types of rice will need a different liquid to rice ratio, and different cooking times. Make sure to follow the packet instructions.

Egg-Fried Rice

**SERVES 2 BIG PEOPLE
& 1 LITTLE PERSON**

300g (2 ½ cups) white
 rice (leftovers, cooked)

2 eggs

1 tbsp light soy sauce

2 spring onions

1 tbsp neutral cooking
 oil (like vegetable oil)

A drizzle of toasted
 sesame oil

Egg-fried rice is one of the best things you can do with leftover rice. It needs to be leftover to make good fried rice and it's a smart move to make extra for this very reason. A good fried rice doesn't need much – high heat, a non-stick wok, eggs, spring onions and light soy sauce. Once you've mastered the trick of moving the rice around, you can start to add other things: prawns, kimchi, leftover roasted meats, various vegetables . . . fried rice can quickly become your go-to, one-dish comfort food meal.

1. Microwave your leftover rice for 45 seconds to soften it a little. This is not an essential step, just a nice thing to do if you have a microwave!

2. In a non-stick wok, heat the oil up to shimmering and add the rice. Flatten it into one layer with a spatula.

3. Meanwhile, slice the spring onions and whip the eggs with the light soy sauce.

4. When the grains of rice start jumping, move the rice around. Add the whites of the spring onion.

5. When the rice is steaming hot, shift it to one side and add the eggs. Let them set for a few seconds, then fold the rice into the egg and keep stir-frying.

6. When the eggs have set, take off the heat and add the greens of the spring onions. Add the sesame oil and stir well.

7. Serve with anything – chilli oil or sauce goes well, or your favourite Chinese dish.

BIG PERSON TIP

It's important not to leave cooked rice at room temperature for longer than necessary. Warm environments can cause cooked rice to grow a bacteria that can make you unwell. Always cool rice down quickly and pop in the fridge as soon as you can – that can be after you've finished your meal. Use within two days.

TaHdig

SERVES 2 BIG PEOPLE
AND 1 LITTLE PERSON

360g (3 ½ cups)
uncooked basmati rice

130g (½ cup) full fat yoghurt

1l (35 fl.oz) water

A pinch of saffron
powder (optional)

½ tsp salt

2 tbsp butter

2 tbsp olive oil

*A non-stick saucepan with
a lid is essential for this.
Use a medium sized pot,
so that the rice layer
is fairly thick.*

Tahdig is the Persian word for
the crispy, crunchy layer you can get
at the bottom of the rice cooking pot, prized
for its satisfying texture. This dish is a visual
feast, but it takes patience and strong nerves
as you can't tell if its worked until you turn
it out. But the results are spectacular and
guaranteed to draw admiring gasps as
you tap your spoon against it.

1. Wash the rice 2 or 3 times. In a large pot bring the water to the boil, add the salt, then add the washed rice. Boil for 7 minutes, then drain in a sieve and rinse with cold water.

2. In the non-stick pot, heat the olive oil on a medium heat. Coat the bottom of the pot until it's shimmering, but not smoking.

3. Mix the yoghurt with half of the rice. Layer this into the pot on top of the oil, taking care to avoid spitting. Ask your Big Person for help if you need it.

4. Layer the rest of the rice on top. Sprinkle the saffron powder if using.

5. Poke holes into the rice layer with a chopstick, about an inch down. Dot the surface with the butter.

6. Wrap the lid with a tea towel. On a low heat, cook for 45 minutes. At this point, carefully prise the bottom to see if you have achieved a golden-brown. If you can't do this, check if the rice is cooked then remove from the heat. This can sometimes take up to 1 hour depending on the brand of rice.

7. This is the scary part that needs help from a Big Person – turning it out! Place a large plate over the saucepan and with oven gloves, quickly flip the rice out onto the plate. You should have a golden, crisp crust, but don't despair if not – the rice is still perfectly edible!

Baked Rice Pudding

**SERVES 2 BIG PEOPLE
& 2 LITTLE PEOPLE**

100g (½ cup) pudding rice,
washed and drained

700ml (25fl. oz.)
semi-skimmed milk

40g (¼ cup) caster sugar

A choice of spices: 6 green
cardamom pods lightly
crushed, 1 cinnamon
stick, 2 star anise *or* a
heavy grating of nutmeg.
You can even combine!

4 tbsp double cream for
serving (optional)

Stone fruit, such as plums,
peaches or nectarines *or*
1 tbsp jam per person

Short-grain rice is ideal for rice pudding. Shorter and stubbier than its basmati or jasmine cousins, short grain rice is starchier, and therefore stickier, making the ideal texture for rice pudding, risottos and sushi. Rice pudding is the stuff of comfort – of cold evenings and warm bowls, rich spices and sticky poached fruits.

1. Add the sugar to the milk, alongside whichever spices you're using, in a small saucepan. If you're using cardamom, crush the pods lightly with your palm to release the seeds before putting them in.

> **TOP TIP**
> *The rice that is labelled 'pudding rice' in the supermarket is absolutely fine to use for risottos and sushi, and it's often much cheaper than the 'real thing'.*

2. Place the milk on the hob on a medium heat, and stir until it's steaming. Take off the heat, and leave the milk to infuse with the lid on for 2 hours or more. You can do this in the morning and leave to infuse (in the fridge) until the evening, if you like.

3. Butter a loaf tin liberally, add the rice, then pour the milk through a sieve into it. Cook for 2 hours in a 140°C (275°F) oven, until the rice grains are soft and it wobbles slightly when you jiggle it (with an oven glove of course!).

4. While the oven is on, get your fruit roasting (if you are including). Halve the fruit, remove the stone and place skin-side down on a baking tray. Depending on size, roast at 200°C (400°F) for around 10–15 minutes, until soft.

5. Serve with a tablespoon of cream splashed over each bowl, and some delicious roasted fruit.

About the Author

Lizzie Mabbott is a self-taught cook, fuelled by an insatiable appetite and a resilience for mishaps. Exploding kimchi and cardboard-like focaccia does not phase her in the slightest in the quest for deliciousness. Currently living in Berlin, chasing after her toddler, she's often dreaming about her homeland and recreating dishes from her childhood in Hong Kong. Her favourite foods include noodles and most rice-based dishes but you won't find her anywhere near a parsnip.

About the Illustrator

Charlotte Dumortier is a freelance illustrator living in Antwerp, Belgium. She has illustrated several books for children including *The Orange, Murphy's Miserable Space Adventures* and *Ella Wil Een Hond*. Her favourite food is noodle soup.